CAROL
OF THE
BELLS

ROB SMALES

Carol of the Bells

Carol of the Bells

Rob Smales

Bad Ideas Press

*This is for all those people who love the holidays . . .
and the rest of us who hate them.*

CAROL OF THE BELLS

Jingle bells, jingle bells,
Jingle all the way . . .
~James Lord Pierpont, 1857

The closing door cut off the invading flow of frigid air with a *thunk* as they entered, loud in the silence that had fallen in the Earle's Inn. Carol gazed nervously at the two dozen faces staring back from the long, low space, pale ovals floating motionless in the gloom of the taproom. Behind her she felt Brian doing the same. Even the tall man behind the dark wooden bar was frozen in the act of cleaning a glass, the rag hanging from the vessel's mouth fluttering in the momentary breeze as he stood gawping. The uncomfortable moment stretched out for the space of four heartbeats. Then five. Six.

Okay, she thought, *this was a mistake. Screw what Brian says, I vote we get the hell out of here right now.*

She shifted her weight, preparing to step backward—right through Brian, if necessary—and return to the car before the seats in their rented Saab had grown cold, when the barman barked out a series of syllables.

"Kineye hilpoo fowks?"

Brian slid around her, stomping the snow from his boots as he stepped forward, speaking confidently in his rough approximation of an English accent.

"We were wondering if you had a room available?"

He'd been working on it the entire time they had been in England, and though she had to admit he'd been getting a little better, Brian's accent was, for the most part, terrible. Still, he

1

sounded like some lord on *Masterpiece Theatre* compared with the barman's accent, so thick it was almost physical. After twelve days of traveling from small English villages to even smaller English villages, however, the whetstone of regional accents had honed her ear to a fine enough edge to suss out the tall man's meaning after merely a moment: *Can I help you folks?*

"Room?" The barman shook his head. "Of *course* we have a room. But I don't think—"

"We'll just have to set it up for you is all." One of the pale faces emerged from the crowd of seated drinkers: a woman, a worn and soiled apron protecting her old-fashioned, high-necked dress from the inevitable spills encountered serving in a bar. She was of an age with the barman—anywhere from thirty to fifty in this dim light—and though she stood ramrod straight, she was as short as he was tall. The way she cut him off without a glance, coupled with his silent, bunching jaw muscles when she did, let Carol make a guess at the relationship: the tall man might have been the landlord, but *this* was the land*lady*, and despite the dress, she wore the pants.

"We just don't see many travelers 'ere, is all," the barkeep said, the polishing rag juddering into a slow rotation within the glass. The low murmur of whispered conversation rose.

Brian, always outgoing and comfortable in his own skin, stepped up to the bar with a hearty "Well, now, mate, that's just what we're looking for."

"What he means is," Carol said, stepping forward herself, hoping the locals wouldn't think Brian was mocking them with his accent, "we're looking for someplace off the beaten path, and the farther off the better. Does that about sum this place up?"

CAROL OF THE BELLS

The barman put down the glass and stood awkwardly for a moment. "We're a fair piece from the city, if that's what you're asking." Then, as if suddenly remembering the conventions, he thrust a hand toward them. "The name's Oliver Barstow. This is my place."

"*Our* place," the woman corrected.

"Our place," he said, rolling his eyes.

"Brian Freeman," said Brian, taking the hand. "This is Carol Friday."

Around them the muted conversations continued, though Carol knew they were still the center of attention.

"Americans?"

Brian's shoulders slumped; he had been working hard on that accent. "Yes. We know we're far from the city; it took us forever to get here. You're nothing more than a dot on the map in the middle of a forest. But that's why we picked you—you're about as far from civilization as we could get without driving right off the island. No offense."

"Well we are remote, I'll give you that," said Mrs. Barstow, ducking under the pass-through to join her husband, absently nudging him out of the way to claim the spot in front of them. "But why were you so set on getting away from the city, if you don't mind my asking?"

"Traditions," Brian answered promptly.

"Beg yer pardon?" Mr. Barstow looked confused, and even his wife blinked.

"Brian had the fantastic idea of getting away from the whole big-city Christmas scene this year," said Carol.

Brian waved a hand. "It's all become *way* too commercialized. It's just—"

The door behind the bar burst open with a sharp jingle of bells, a wooden cask butting its way through, followed by a large man pushing it along on a rickety wooden hand-truck.

"All right, Da, here's the . . ."

As the words trailed off, the hand truck slipped from the man's grip and the cask thudded to the floor.

Oliver Barstow's eyes went wide. "Careful, you clums—"

"Oh, dear, did you hurt your toes?" Mrs. Barstow interrupted. The man merely stared at Carol, mouth hanging slightly open. Mrs. Barstow raised her voice, enunciating clearly. "Did you hurt yourself?"

"What? Oh, no, Mum. I'm fine. Who's the pretty—I mean, the new people?"

He looked to be somewhat older than the Americans, maybe twenty-five or twenty-six, but something about unabashed curiosity made him seem younger, as though the question had come from an over-large child, and while he asked about both of them, his eyes never left Carol.

"You stop asking your questions now," said Mrs. Barstow, "and go open—"

She looked at Carol, rather than Brian, with a raised eyebrow, and Carol felt a moment of dread. Since they'd left the city behind, they'd met ever-increasing disapproval: an obviously unmarried couple sharing a room. The deeper into the boonies they got, the worse it was, and they were about as deep now as they could get. Just the night before, they'd had to argue with a landlady who'd insisted they take two rooms. Strike that: *Carol* had argued. Brian had folded like a well-used paper bag, but Carol had refused to yield—in part because it wasn't in her nature, but also because all of the disapproving stares seemed to be aimed, not at Brian, but at *her*. Then, as now, though Brian asked for the room, Carol caught the evil eye. She stared back at Mrs. Barstow, readying for a fight, but determined not to fire the first shot.

Mrs. Barstow smiled. "One room?" The hubbub of conversation died away.

Braced as she was, as if expecting a gale, Carol nearly stumbled when it did not appear. The landlady's smile was wide and ingratiating, and her voice had been, if anything, cheerful. Her eyes still looked hard, though, and the silence in the room spoke of *something*, but Carol didn't know *what*. Curiosity? Tension? The little woman ignored the crowd, however, gazing at Carol with that raised eyebrow, awaiting a response. Still bracing, more than half-expecting it to be a trap leading to a lecture about morals, Carol nodded. The little landlady turned back to her son.

"—the room top of the stairs. I'll bring our guests along in a few."

The big man didn't move. Mr. Barstow gave his shoulder a gentle nudge. "Go on, Simon. Do as your mother says. I'll stow the cask."

Simon tore his eyes from Carol, spun on his heel with another loud jingle, and bustled back through the door. Watching him go, Carol saw he wore red trousers with a white shirt and—this was the part that really caught her eye—bunches of bright, silver bells at his knees and ankles.

"And you take off those Solstice clothes before you get them dirty!" Mrs. Barstow called. "You know you won't be . . ." but her words became a sigh as the door swung closed.

From the crowd behind them came a hoarse whisper, the speaker obviously intending to be overheard: "Looks like Simon's got himself a new girlfriend."

"Sorry 'bout that," Barstow said. "He's a good boy, but he's a bit . . . well, he's plenty big, but"—the man touched the side of his head—"he ain't never gonna be all growed up, if you know what I mean. And you *are* a pretty thing, you don't mind my saying, miss."

"That's all right," Carol said, flattered and embarrassed. "I don't—"

"Was he," said Brian, squinting at the barman, "dressed for Morris dancing?"

Carol turned to Brian, annoyed at the interruption. "What the hell is Morris dancing?"

"It's a type of English folk dancing," he said. "Dating back to . . . well, they're not sure how far back. Some say all the way to the Druids."

"Done your research, I see," said Mr. Barstow.

"Well, that *is* the reason we're here."

The tall Englishman looked confused again, and Carol felt her irritation at Brian, with his single-minded, know-it-all attitude, slip up a notch, though she kept her tone warm for the barman's sake. "We came to England, and then to your hard-to-find little village, looking for the oldest, most authentic holiday traditions we can find."

"We were in Austria for Krampusnacht." Brian motioned dismissively. "Even in the little town we were in, the whole thing was nearly as commercialized as an American Christmas. Kids waving Krampus dolls and smiling as the parade passed—they weren't taking the *tradition* seriously, just the fun. Even Morris dancing, as old as it is"—he held up a hand to the barman—"and it *is* ancient, don't get me wrong, but even *that's* become tamed, with a national bureau you have to register with in order for your team to be 'official.'"

He made finger quotes around the word to showcase his disgust.

"I was a little excited at your mention of the solstice, but if Morris dancing is all you—"

"But he's not dressed for Morris dancing," said Mrs. Barstow, indignation hardening her voice. "Tomorrow starts the solstice, and those are his Solsticeniht clothes."

She shot a look toward Mr. Barstow. "Which he shouldn't be wearing. He knows they won't let him take part." She offered the Americans a somewhat embarrassed smile. "They say he's not *mature* enough."

Behind her, Mr. Barstow touched the side of his head again, with a nod.

"Solsticeniht?" said Brian. "I've never even heard of a—"

"Predates Morris dancing, you see," said the little woman, chin high with pride. "Where the Morris dance springs from, if you must know. The rest of the world may have forgotten the Solsticeniht, but we haven't."

Brian stared at the landlady, his faux-British accent slipping away entirely in his surprise. "Do you mean to tell me that this Solsticeniht is what the *Druids* . . ."

Her little head gave one sharp nod. "Just so, sir."

The bar had gone silent again, the crowd caught up in the discussion, but here a low rumble rose up once more, the locals apparently pleased to have surprised this upstart Yank.

"Can we take part?"

The rumbling stilled, and Brian looked about, concerned he may have made a faux pas. "I only meant—"

"Oh." Mrs. Barstow's words were loud and clear through her wide smile. "What a *wonderful* idea! I'm sure we could find *something* for you to do. Tomorrow night, I think."

"Room's open, Mum," said Simon, jingling through the door again to stare, with puppy-like adoration, in Carol's direction.

"Well, then," said Mrs. Barstow, bustling back under the pass-through and beckoning them toward a door at the rear of the taproom. "Let's get you two into your room, shall we? You're in for a long day tomorrow—and an even longer night."

"The longest night!" called her husband as they passed through the door, the phrase echoed by several in the crowd, like some sort of call and response.

That sounds pretty promising, Carol thought, following their strangely solicitous hostess up the stairs. *I just hope Brian's not setting himself up for another disappointment.*

"You can skip your run for just one day, can't you?"

The sun was just cresting the trees, and Carol stood in the semi-dark, caught in the act of tiptoeing toward the door, running shoes in hand, and looked at the shape under the blankets.

"You're awake?"

The shape thrashed and Brian sat up, a scarecrow-headed silhouette.

"I'm excited about today. This is a festival I've never even *heard* of—it's why we came to Europe in the first place. The marathon's not until April, right? Why not take a day—*one day*—to relax and have fun?"

Carol stood a moment more, listening to the inn coming to life below them. She remembered the state of the road they'd driven on to get to this place; it was runnable, but barely: potholed and not plowed well. Skipping a run went against the grain with her, and she did have a set of those ice spikes to strap onto her running shoes, but a twisted ankle or wrenched knee could put her weeks out of training. She puffed a sigh, but bent and swapped her sneakers for hiking boots: better suited for the snow.

"Fine," she said, sitting on the edge of the bed to pull on a boot. "Can I at least go for a walk and check out the village? We barely saw anything last night."

The mattress shuddered as Brian wrestled his stocky frame to its edge and threw his legs over the side.

"I'll come with you." His grin was huge and infectious in the growing light. "This is going to be *great*!"

The day was filled with celebration, and Carol found herself enjoying the lovely, old-fashioned hominess of it all. Each door in the village bore a wreath of evergreen, pinecones, and mistletoe. Children skipped about wearing crowns of holly, the green leaves and red berries offering a splash of color to cap their threadbare and obviously handed-down finery. Songs cropped up everywhere, villagers singing with each other like they were in some sort of holiday musical.

Most of the songs sounded to Carol like unintelligible gibberish. Mrs. Barstow, having taken some time away from the inn to accompany her guests from across the pond, explained, with her spine-straining pride, that they'd been handed down from the time of the Druids, before English, as a language, even *was*.

"They're songs to the land, and the sun, and the day, reminding them to come back to us after the long slumber ahead. The land has been sleeping, a little deeper each day, and if she falls too far she may never wake. We're telling the land that we need her, reminding her that it's time to start to wake up now, before the world is swathed in everlasting darkness."

As the sun reached its zenith, the entire village gathered at the tall evergreen in the center of the town square, the open space across which the Earl's Inn sat facing the small, spare church. The younger children began dancing around the tree, reminding Carol of a maypole, though they all moved in the same direction. Singing a song of gibberish again, one by one they began throwing small things into a fire burning at the base of the tree, the blaze attended by an ancient stick of a woman in an antique black dress. Carol saw berries and small foodstuffs arc into the flames, but there was an occasional toy as well, small rough dolls and wooden swords, all of it feeding the fire.

The older children joined in then, and after them the adults. Carol and Brian were pulled into the dance, villagers tugging them along despite Carol's embarrassed protestations, though Brian went eagerly. They sang along as best they could, Brian with his usual enthusiasm, Carol merely mouthing the words, making occasional, approximate sounds, much as she had in church as a child. When the time came that the people about her were tossing their items—their sacrifices, she assumed—into the fire, Carol found herself digging into a pocket and pulling out the first thing she found. Caught up in the moment, she was surprised to see her house keys spinning toward the pyre.

Going to need a new set of those, she thought, chagrined at getting so swept up in the festivities, then caught Brian from the corner of her eye flinging something that looked suspiciously like his full money clip into the flames.

"What the hell are you—" she began, but the hands about her nudged and pulled, voices singing imperatively, and she spun on in the dance, clumsily following along while trying to keep an eye on her potentially insane boyfriend.

The ancient woman finally entered the dance, making a single circuit about the trunk before returning to stand by the fire, head bowed and muttering. The circle began to break up then, dancers leaving it in the reverse of how they'd entered, the adults dancing away, then the older children, until finally there was but one small child still dancing, a girl surely no more than three. When she realized she was out there alone, the toddler pirouetted away from the tree, spinning faster and faster until dizziness overtook her and she fell, giggling, into the well-trodden snow.

The song ended, not petering out in dribs and drabs, but the entire village stopping on the same note, as if in response to some hidden signal. Without applause, or even congratulating each other on a job well done, everyone Carol could see merely went about their business, as if nothing special had just happened—though they all now wore similar grins of satisfaction. She spotted their landlady shuffling toward the inn, and hurried to catch up.

"So is that it, then, Mrs. Barstow? That's the solstice festival, or whatever you call it?"

"That was the Renewal Dance, my dear," said the older woman. "For Solsticedæg. Solsticedæg started at dawn and goes on until dusk. Solsticeniht starts when the sun goes down." Her eyes grew a trifle hard again, but, as it had the night before, her smile remained intact. "Besides, did you hear any bells?"

Carol recalled Simon's clothes of the night before, the bells he'd worn at knees and ankles, and shook her head.

"Well just remember then: Solstice *Day* ain't over, and Solstice *Night* ain't begun, until you and your young man have heard the bells."

They had been nearing the inn as they talked, and at their approach Simon emerged, holding the door open for his mother. He had been in time to catch the tail end of his mother's words, and as he stared at Carol she watched his expression change from familiar puppy-dog adoration to one, inexplicably, of sorrow.

"Wasn't that *some*thing?"

Carol turned to find Brian, ruddy-faced with cold and drink and still out of breath from the dance, trotting up behind her. "I mean, that was just fan*tas*tic, wasn't it?"

She turned back to Simon, meaning to ask if something was wrong, only to find the unattended door swinging shut with a quiet *thud*.

"One second," she said over her shoulder, moving to follow the simple young man, but at a sudden flash of memory she reversed, rounding on Brian again.

"Was that your *money* you threw on the fire?"

By the time she entered the inn once more, a severely chastened—and, it turned out, quite tipsy—Brian in tow, Simon's changing expression had completely slipped her mind.

Luckily the Barstows insisted that food and drink for the young couple were on the house that day (Brian *had* thrown his money clip into the fire, making that a slightly more than two hundred dollar dance, thank you *very* much), fair recompense, they insisted, for Carol and Brian's taking part in the upcoming ceremony.

"We don't get many visitors here," said Mrs. Barstow, setting a salver of bread and cheese on the table. "You two being here, well, you make this year special."

It didn't take Brian long, once finding out his drinks were on the house, to forgive himself for the money clip fiasco. Soon he was standing by the fire with the other men, discussing things he knew nothing about, or following them out to celebrate in the square, mug after mug of home-brewed beer sprouting from his fist.

Carol remained at their table, simmering about the money, and nervous about her part in the upcoming ceremony. People stopped by her table occasionally, most expressing their thanks for taking part in Solsticeniht before moving on. Though Carol wasn't drinking with Brian's unabashed abandon, Mrs. Barstow kept her wine glass topped up so she was never quite sure how much she'd had. Eventually, lulled by the constant singing, bored with waiting for dusk to come, and unused to drinking wine all day, even in moderation, her eyelids grew heavy, then heavier, until the sandman finally crept in, the world's gentlest mugger, and stole her consciousness away.

CAROL OF THE BELLS

"Time to wake up, dear."

Carol opened her eyes. Mrs. Barstow stood before her, hands folded primly, teeth bared in a wide smile.

"Wha—?" Carol said, confused, the taste of old wine sour on her tongue.

"It's time, dear," the older woman said through her grin. "They're all waiting for us in the square."

"Waiting?" Carol looked about the taproom, finding it empty. The afternoon came back to her: the dance about the tree, holding court at her table, and her ever-full wine glass.

Carol rose and took two faltering steps: the long time spent in the wooden chair had left her unsteady on her feet.

"I'm not drunk," she told Mrs. Barstow, worried the woman might somehow think less of her, but the landlady merely nodded and took her arm, steadying her as they walked across the taproom. Carol was struck again by the emptiness, the silence and shadows combining to make this place of friendly talk and good cheer now seem cold, almost sinister. She shook her head, trying to lose this strange feeling of dread along with the shreds of sleep-fog still clinging to her brain.

"You said 'they're waiting.' Who's waiting?"

"Oh, now, dear," said the little woman, turning the handle and pulling open the inn's front door. "I did say 'all,' didn't I?"

Carol's eyes widened, and her voice emerged as a whisper. "*Holy shit.*"

In the time Carol had been asleep the sun had gone down, and though the villagers remained in the square, they no longer cavorted or sang; instead they lined the square, silently ringing the open area around the great tree. Man, woman, and child, each carried a candle, flickering beacons all but lost in the wash of silver from the nearly full moon, hanging in the sky above like the blind eye of an some ancient god. In the center of the circle, though she could not see its base through the wall of bodies, the fire in front of the giant fir tree still burned, stoked to the status of bonfire now, the flames leaping higher than a man.

As they stepped through the door and into view, the great ring burst into song, as if they had all been waiting for just this moment.

"What's going on?"

Ignoring the question, Mrs. Barstow maintained her grip on Carol's arm, tugging her forward. The wall of candle-bearers parted, allowing Mrs. Barstow to lead Carol into the ring before it closed behind them. Once inside the circle, Carol saw it was not as empty as she'd assumed: lined up before the bonfire, their backs toward her, were a half-dozen men, all dressed in what Mrs. Barstow had referred to as Simon's solstice clothes: white shirts with red trousers, bunches of bells at their knees and ankles. She looked about the circle as they approached the men; all about her, singing villagers stared back.

"What's going—" she began, nervous at being the center of attention once more, but her small guide raised a hand almost absently with a "shhhh."

The villagers' song rose as the two women moved to stand between the line of red-and-white garbed men and the flames. Looking at her feet, viscerally aware of the scrutiny of the entire village, Carol tried not to trip over anything in the almost black-and-white world created by the night and snow. She had a moment to consider the low, rumbling chant, similar to the songs from that afternoon only in the fact that she didn't understand a word of it.

CAROL OF THE BELLS

*This afternoon the songs were all happy—or they **sounded** happy, at least. This, though, this feels . . . different.*

Then she looked up at the row of men before her, seeing them from the front for the first time.

Oh my God!

They were indeed dressed as Simon had been the day before, in white tunics and red pants, large bell-laden black boots planted firmly in the snow as they stood motionless before the fire. Their faces, however, were huge, misshapen things, hard to make out in the moonlight, though the occasional snap-*pop* of exploding pockets of pitch gave off flashes of brighter light, revealing the large, deformed countenances of demons before her.

Masks, like in Austria.

Giant, inhuman faces stared at her like the ones they'd seen on Krampusnacht, but where those had all been different, each its own stylized version of Krampus, these six were all the same. Great mouths hung open in obvious hunger, showing huge, square, stone-like teeth. Atop sharp, jutting cheekbones were great eyeholes, deep pits of shadow, the eyes themselves invisible. Over these black sockets hung expansive brows, smooth where the lower portions of the faces looked rough-hewn. Great snarls of stylized hair topped these grotesqueries, thick twists jutting this way and that, so convoluted Carol took them at first to be snakes, much like Medusa's fabled serpentine locks; until, that is, an exploding pocket of pitch brightened the night enough for her to make out the knotted roots below and the straighter, leafy shoots above. She saw, too, the color: each mask was blood red, though in the shadows of night, illuminated by that great, dead eye, they all appeared quite black.

The land! she realized with a start. *From their big stony teeth up to the plants at the top! They're the land!*

Every voice halted on the same syllable, as if the song had been shut off by flipping a switch.

"Quit it, you assholes!"

The familiar voice was loud in the sudden silence, and Carol turned to see the candle circle closing behind three wrestling forms. A pair of burly men dragged Brian forward, clutching his arms to yank him through the snow. They cast him roughly to the ground, then turned without a word, marching back to take positions in the circle, while Brian struggled to his feet.

"Jesus Christ, are you okay?" Carol took his elbow to help him rise, but he shook her off, turning to shout at his former captors' retreating backs.

"Is that how you treat a fucking *guest*, assholes? Seriously? How am I supposed to—"

He broke off, catching sight of the masked figures for the first time.

"What the *hell*?"

"Are you okay?" Carol said again. He spun to face her, outrage plain on his face.

"Sure! I'm just frigging tip-top! I was sitting there having a drink with those guys—just having a fine time—when this bell rang, like a church bell, you know? The next thing I know, those two walking ringpieces grabbed me and forced me to drink this, this . . . I don't know *what* it was, but this *stuff* that tasted like stewed goat shit, and I threw up all over the place."

"Oh," she said. "Is that what . . .?" she indicated the dark spatters marking the front of his jacket.

CAROL OF THE BELLS

"*That's* from the *second* time they made me drink the stuff, on our way here. They said it would sober me up, but for Christ's sake, I wasn't even—"

"*Cwildseten cóm æt eorð!*"

The ancient stick-woman, no longer in black, but robed now in white and red to match the six masked men, came into view.

"*Nihtglóm, ælenge ond ceald.*"

Hidden until now by the great bonfire, she marched about the blaze, arms outstretched as if in entreaty to the candle-bearers encircling them, spouting words of the same gibberish as the songs of that afternoon. Brian turned to Carol.

"What the *fuck* is going—"

"Night has come to the land," said Mrs. Barstow, stepping between them and the ancient woman, addressing them in her clear, penetrating voice.

"*You* can tell us—" Brian began again, but she went on as if he hadn't spoken, standing with her hands folded like a schoolgirl reciting something before her class, and Carol realized what she was doing: translating the elder's words for them. Brian fell silent beside her.

"Darkness, long and cold. And the land does sleep, the deep sleep of the weary. And weary she should be, having sustained us for yet another year in her long, long life, as we wend our tiny ways across her great, broad back. But, tiny as we may seem to the great Stone Mother, we must not let her forget us. We must not let her sleep of winter grow too deep, for once she fell so far she could not rouse herself. She slept for many years as the ice and snow covered her back in a thick blanket of cold and hunger. It was a time of death for many who looked to her for sustenance: those of beast and bird, and those of bark and root, and many, many of the children of Man did perish as unending winter covered the land.

"We must not let the Land sleep too deeply. We will not. We will waken her with offerings of love and of loss. The offering was begun with the sacrifice of things small and dear; now we will complete the offering with the sacrifice of that thing most precious to us all: life itself, a sacrifice of bone, and meat, and blood, to feed the Stone Mother. To prod her into wakefulness for yet another year!"

"What the hell is this?" Brian shouted. "What's going on? What 'sacrifice?'"

"Why, you, of course." The landlady's face was stone as Brian blinked in confusion, and Carol felt a moan slip up her throat to fog the air before her. "Your bones for the fire. Your meat for our bellies. Your blood to feed the Stone Mother, and to wake the land."

Carol looked at this woman who had answered their questions all day, and couldn't force more than a terrified whisper. "What are you talking about?"

Small, dark eyes shifted from Brian to her.

"I'm talking about a hunt, my dear. You run." She indicated the red-and-white figures standing silent in the firelight. "They follow. And when they catch you, your blood will wake the land before it's too late."

Carol's gaze raked the waiting men—the hunters—and saw that not one of them carried a gun, a bow, or anything she might have associated with hunting. Instead, each had two weapons thrust through his belt: to one side a cleaver, to the other a broad-bladed knife.

Jesus Christ, she thought. *They're butcher's tools.*

"Thank you for offering yourselves as you did," Mrs. Barstow went on. "It saved us the trouble of having to go out today to find a pair of 'volunteers.'"

Her voice dropped to a whisper. "You've made tonight very special."

Carol turned toward Brian, hoping he'd say something, offer some argument against what was happening to them, even one of his pedantic explanations about it all being symbolic rather than real, but her breath froze in her throat as she saw the elder woman, all but forgotten after finishing her ancient recitation, step up behind him. A wiry arm swung, and Brian cried out in surprise and pain as her knife passed through the meat of his thigh. Blood spattered the snow, black on white in the silvery moonlight. Carol cried out, staggering as the world spun, the edges of her vision darkening in the precursor to a dead faint. A sudden razor's edge of pain snapped the world back into sharp focus, and she turned, clutching her hip, to see Mrs. Barstow stepping nimbly away, the knife in her hand stained as black as the snow.

The blood seeping between Carol's fingers was warm in the winter night. "Why?" she whispered.

"To mark you for the hunt," said the landlady; then her solemnity broke into a wide smile. "You'll have a five-minute head start, but we wouldn't want you actually getting *away* now, would we?" Behind her, Carol heard the snow squeak and crunch as the hunters shifted restlessly.

"What if we won't run?" Brian drew himself up, as much as he was able while squeezing his wounded leg, chin raised in defiance. "What if we refuse?"

"You'll run," Mrs. Barstow said, quiet and serious. "You always do."

A pair of the hunters stepped forward holding what looked to be thin branches stripped of twigs and bark. One of the men swung his switch in a wide arc, and it made an audible whip-*crack* against Brian's denim-clad buttocks. Brian howled, his hands leaving his thigh to grip his backside: the second man's swing deftly avoided the tail of Brian's coat to catch him across his clutching fingers, and the howl became a shriek. The first man raised his switch again as another pair of hunters stepped toward Carol, one of them already testing the night air with his wooden weapon, eagerly swiping it back and forth with a *whick-whick-whick*.

They ran.

CAROL OF THE BELLS

"Where . . . are we . . . going?"

Brian's words came between great gasping breaths as he limped through the snow. Carol tossed a response over one shoulder.

"Away."

"Have . . . to do something . . . about my leg."

Her feet churned to a halt and she turned to find him already stopped, bent at the waist and gagging. She wished, for what felt like the thousandth time since leaving that flame-filled village square, that she had been more insistent that he go running with her more often. Or even at all.

He still gripped his thigh, his whole hand glistening black in the moonlight. She checked her own hip and found her jeans stained with blood, though not nearly the amount showing on Brian's leg. It might have just been that the old woman was a particularly evil bitch, but Carol suspected her incipient fainting spell may have saved her some serious damage: her sudden stagger had made her a moving target, while Brian, standing firmly on both feet, had taken a deeper cut.

"Let me see."

She knelt in the snow to peer at his leg, but he had smeared the blood about, and she couldn't see much. Ignoring the sensation of creeping worms in her gut, she carefully probed the rent in the denim with her fingers; then nearly vomited when she felt something warm and meaty and realized her fingertips were *inside* his leg. She turned her head away, pulling air in through her nose and pushing it out through her mouth in a runner's rhythm, trying to calm her churning stomach. All about them the moonlight fell upon trees thrusting up through snow, the great white orb blanketing the scene in a soft glow, reminding her of a picture postcard, or one of those beautiful landscape images used for computer desktops. She glanced sideways at Brian's leaking leg and nearly laughed aloud, though it wouldn't have been a happy sound.

"This is, uh, this looks pretty bad," she said, finally looking up at him. "You still have that pocket knife?"

"Yeah, but—"

"Give it to me and open your coat."

"But I—"

"Just do it, Bri."

She unfolded the tiny blade, sharp as a razor though only two inches long, as he unzipped his coat. She grabbed the lower edge of his button-down shirt, cut, then yanked hard, tearing off a strip of the cotton blend. She tied it around his thigh while he zipped up, and he grunted with pain when she pulled the knot tight.

"Think that'll work?" he said, gingerly testing weight on the leg.

"Dunno," she said, standing and folding the knife into her own pocket. "But it's what they always do in those stupid man-movies you make me watch. Come on, we're going to have to—"

She froze, listening. She thought she'd heard—

Bells. Sleigh bells jingling rhythmically, as if attached to running feet. The bright, cheery sound drove a cold spike through her heart, the quick shot of adrenaline that flooded her system chasing her nausea away in a single second.

"We have to move!"

"What? Why—"

He broke off, listening too, and when the sound registered he took two faltering steps before looking back at her with wild eyes.

"Come on!" he said. "We have to go. Where?"

His eyes darted this way and that as he took in the same scenery she'd used to quell her stomach; she thought it was the first time he'd actually stopped to think since they'd dragged him into the candle circle. His eyes finished their dance and settled on her once more as she started to move, passing him at a jog, forcing him to keep up.

"Where can we go?" he said, falling into step behind her. "What can we do?"

"We can keep running."

"But to where?" he asked, already panting. "The nearest town . . . has to be . . . ten miles."

Ten miles. She could make ten miles, even in the boots she wore, if only she knew which direction to take. She looked around again: nothing but trees and snow and moon-drenched sky.

I have no idea where I am, no clue what I'm doing out here. Maybe I could find the road, but I don't even know how to do that. *Besides, there's—*

"Wait! I can't . . ."

Brian was struggling now, already falling behind. She paused to let him catch up, then watched as he staggered to a halt and fell to one knee, vomiting into the snow.

I'm never going to get anywhere with him slowing me down, she thought, *but I couldn't—*

25

"Please." Brian looked up from his steaming little puddle of bile and used beer with an expression of abject terror, holding a hand toward her in supplication. "You can't leave me. Please!"

She cringed inside at having her speculation echoed so closely. Had her thoughts shown so plainly on her face?

"No," she said, stepping close to help him to his feet. "Of course not. But we have to keep moving, Brian. We *have* to."

He glanced back as the sound of the bells came again. They seemed closer this time, louder in the silence of the great winter forest.

"Christ! How did they find us so fast?" He looked at her in sudden inspiration. "We could find someplace to hide! You know, just hole up and let them run on past, then run the other way! Maybe under these trees—"

He started away, turning toward a nearby fir, its wide spread of branches forming a canopy that touched the snow, but she used her grip on his arm to yank him back around.

"Same answer to both." She pointed to the ground behind them; the ankle-deep snow between the trees was unbroken but for the obvious tracks of a couple in panicked flight. "All they have to do is follow the dotted line, and they'll come right to us, no matter where we go. All we can do is keep ahead of them, not let them catch up. We can run," she said, pulling him into motion, aiming between the trees where the running might be easier. "But we can't hide."

With a muffled sob, he lumbered into a jog, following her through the forest.

Behind them, rhythmic bells jingled cheerily in the night.

They ran. They ran from tree to tree, looking for the thinnest snow, seeking out the easiest path. Carol's hip throbbed with each step, draining her strength with the constant pain: she had no idea how Brian was going on, with his deeper wound, but he did. Sometimes he staggered ahead of her, but most often he brought up the rear. Gasping and panting, he'd wave her on when she looked back, concerned that she was leaving him behind, haunted by guilt from those thoughts of making it on her own.

They ran.

They ran downhill, following the terrain the way water flows, through the path of least resistance, in an effort to get somewhere, *anywhere*, just as long as that place was safe and sound and filled with sane people who celebrated Christmas, and nothing else. They weren't on the side of a mountain, however, but in a flat forest; for every slope they charged down they found a corresponding incline on the other side, losing whatever precious advantage they may have gained struggling out of dips and hollows, sometimes slipping back one step for every two, clinging to each other for support.

And behind, ever following, came the bells, the sharp tones flying to them on the night breeze. Sometimes they pulled ahead of their pursuers, thanks to either a more lengthy downhill slope or simple dumb luck, and there would be nothing but blessed silence around them; but every time they paused to rest, stopping to let Brian catch his breath, it wouldn't be long before the tinkle of the bells would return, a silvery snake of sound, slithering toward them through the trees, and they would be off again. Carol wasn't sure how Brian kept going—she'd been sure he couldn't go another step at their first rest, ten minutes into the chase, and now it had been an hour, at least—but he did, staggering on in his fatigue, letting her lead him as he simply put one foot in front of the other.

Then he fell.

Carol dashed back to where he was struggling to his feet and discovered the problem: the snow's smooth surface had hidden a depression in the ground, and Brian had stepped, without warning, into a knee-deep hole. She helped him up to more solid ground and led him, limping, through the trees.

"You should go on," he muttered through cold-numbed lips, staring at the ground rather than her, just trying to stay in motion.

"What?"

"I was wrong before. I'm not . . . gonna make it."

He raised his eyes to meet hers as she jogged alongside him, and she saw he'd changed over the past hour, though she'd been too busy running to notice. When he'd first had to stop, where she'd bandaged his leg, his eyes and voice were filled with terror, afraid she was going to abandon him to his fate and run on. Now, however, his voice was a hoarse thing, without inflection, and his eyes were filled with resignation. Tears ran down a face that was dead calm.

"You should go on without me."

"What? No! I—"

Her right foot came down on nothing, plunging through the snow—then caught up hard against the ground, much lower than she'd expected. She managed to tuck one shoulder and roll as she fell in a hidden depression of her own. Snow skittered down the back of her collar and pants as she rolled, the sudden, sharp chill stealing her breath. She scrambled to her feet, batting at her coat, trying to shake the invading crystals of cold out the bottom of her shirt, and nearly fell again as her knee gave way.

"You see." Brian stood swaying, shoulders slumped, arms hanging loose like a marionette at rest, watching with his dead eyes. "You need to go on. Maybe I can slow them down or something."

She stared at him for a moment, wondering just who this was, standing here in Brian's clothes and trying to do the noble thing, then had to look away as the thoughts came.

(It's just like I thought. He's slowing me down.)

She tried to push them away,

(if they caught him, then at least two of them would have to take him to the village)

but it was like trying to smooth out a bubble under new wallpaper:

(that'd be two less out here hunting me.*)*

She pressed one down only to have another pop up in a different place.

(I should *leave him!)*

She inspected her leg, working the knee, testing it. Focusing on it—on *anything*—besides those thoughts. "You really *have* been watching too many of those stupid man-movies of yours. It'd be diff—"

The word caught in her throat. She swallowed, clearing the way.

"It'd be different if we weren't trying to cover rough ground in this damn snow!" She kicked at the ankle-deep whiteness, instantly regretting it as pain in both knee and hip flared. "If we could find the road it would be different. We could make better time—maybe even flag down a car or something."

29

"So let's find the road."

"How?" Her hands flopped in a helpless gesture. "We don't even know where—"

"Climb a tree." His words were still dead, inflectionless, and it took a moment for their meaning to sink in. She looked at him in confusion.

"What?" Carol detected a flicker about the eyes that suggested Brian had *almost* offered her the ghost of a smile.

"Climb up,"—he pointed toward the trunk they stood next to—"and look for an open lane between the trees. Chances are it's a road. Or a river. But I don't remember anyone mentioning a big river anywhere around here."

She stared at him a moment, then looked about, knowing they'd already been there too long, that men with knives and cleavers were gaining on them every second.

"We don't have time."

His expression never changed. "You have any other ideas?"

She held her breath, listening for another moment, heard nothing but Brian's breathing, the creak of frozen branches in the light breeze—and then she was climbing, fingers stiff with cold screaming as she forced them to grip branch after branch. Her boots scrabbled at the trunk, seeking purchase as, in her hurry, they missed limbs. She bit back curses as she stubbed fingertips on branches, closing her eyes against the smaller branches and twigs that clawed at her face and body as she forced her way upward, as though the tree itself were trying to hold her back.

The point at which the tiny branches stopped scratching her seemed to coincide with the height where the limbs no longer looked like they'd support her weight. The safe and sane part of her—the Carol from just yesterday—tried to pull back on the reins and get her to stop, but the Carol of today, the Carol of right now, would not be stopped; she climbed higher, hands and feet close to the trunk. Finally the branches surrounding her thinned enough and she could see out over the forest. She swiveled her head this way and that, searching the treetops eagerly, looking for a long gap, a meandering corridor between the trees that would signal the road, give them a direction to go in that just might lead to salvation—

—but she saw nothing, no break in the forest that could be anything other than a small clearing here or there.

"No," she muttered, the words oozing from between clenched teeth. "No, there has to be *something*!"

In desperation she twisted herself about the thin trunk—no thicker than her own calf, she had climbed so high. She looked down as she swung about, repositioned her feet carefully on the thin branches she prayed would continue supporting her weight, then raised her chin to look out over the forest once more.

Her breath caught in a guttural gasp as her heart froze.

"No," she whispered. "No-no-no."

There, in a huge clearing all its own barely a half mile away, was the village. In all their running, and following the flow of the land, the land had betrayed them, leading them in a twisting, turning half-circle, to a place no farther from their starting point than could be covered in a comfortable, ten-minute stroll. Even the bonfire still burned, the flat, snow-covered planes of rooftops on the far side of the square lit up by the flames, the snow showing red in the night like flickering pools of blood.

No wonder they find us so easily.

She was shinnying down the tree now, nearly falling in her haste to get to the ground and start running again.

We're an easy walk from home for these guys—they could track us in shifts, we're so close.

She was halfway down when she thought to warn Brian that they had to get moving—they had to choose a direction and just run straight—but he beat her to it.

"Run!" His whisper floated up through the tree, harsh yet quiet in the night. "Run the other way!"

She stopped climbing to peer down through the branches and saw his upturned face, a dim oval above his dark coat in the shadows beneath the tree. He was leaning his hands against the trunk, but the way he shifted his head about she wasn't sure he could make her out amidst the limbs.

"What?"

"Did you hear me?" More than a whisper now, nearly a hoarse bark. "Wait until they come for me, then run the other way! Do it!"

"What the hell are you—" she began, but then she heard it, and her words stopped as if her whisper itself were afraid.

Bells. Jingling bells, already close and getting closer. The oval disappeared as Brian turned, looking back the way they had come, then reappeared as he whispered up to her as sharply as he dared.

"The other way! Run! Live!"

Then he was gone, staggering off through the snow, and she heard him loose a loud sob. The bells jingled to a halt for a moment, then started up again amidst shouting voices:

"I heard them!"

"Up ahead there! There!"

CAROL OF THE BELLS

"Come on!"

The rhythmic jingle of jogging became the hard *chink-chink-chink* of sprinting, a whole leg's worth of bells all clapping in unison with every pounding stride, each note a silver spike driving into Carol's ears. She clung to the trunk as the hunters, following Brian's tracks, passed right beneath her perch. She squeezed tight to the tree, trying to mold herself to the trunk and into invisibility, holding her breath, willing her very heart to stop beating in case they might hear it pounding against her ribs.

But they filed on past without looking up, intent on the prey they had in their sights, red-and-white figures with oversized, grinning heads, every one holding both knife and cleaver as if anxious to put them to use. Breaths rasped inside their masks, the headdresses making their excited shouts sound hollow and eerie.

One of them was laughing.

Brian heard them coming, or maybe caught sight of them passing under the tree, for just as the last of the masked butchers swept by the trunk, Carol heard a wail echo across the field, a sound of fear and despair cut short by lack of breath. The *chink-chink-chink* of the sprinting bells stormed on through the night as Carol slid down, practically falling in her haste to flee. She hit the ground hard, her strained knee giving out again, and rolled, half-somersaulting before dragging herself back to the tree, crab-walking through the snow until her shoulders slammed into the bark. She moved without looking, trying only to get behind cover lest one of them turn at the sound of her fall and spot her. Carol tried to hold her breath again, terrified of being overheard, but the gasps would not stop coming, her whole body jerking against the rough surface as her fingers

33

clawed in the snow, a fingernail catching a root and peeling back to the quick as she pressed herself harder against the trunk.

She needn't have worried: the stabbing song of the bells went on even after Brian's screams started. Carol told herself not to look, to do as Brian had said and run, but her body refused to listen. She rose to her knees, turning to face the tree, and though she begged herself to push off and dash away just as fast as she could, fingers gripped the rough bark once again as she peered around the trunk and into the clearing beyond.

Brian lay supine in the snow, strangely quiescent, his screams reduced to moans and repeating "please, God," over and over. He lay still and cried as two of his captors stood facing each other across him, arms spread and chanting, much as the old woman at the bonfire had. The other four formed a sort of square about them, chanting and dancing, spinning in place, the bells on their legs a constant sound.

She had looked just in time to see the chant end, all six men clapping their hands once in unison. Then, moving in a concerted fashion that bespoke much practice, one man stood before them, arms spread wide and eyes heavenward, murmuring words Carol couldn't make out, while five of them hoisted Brian into the air, one on each limb, one with arms wrapped about his torso. He cried out as they lifted him, and as they swiveled him about to hang upside down, his hair nearly brushing the snow, she saw why: dark gashes in his coat and jeans marked where they had slashed the tendons at shoulders and hips, rendering his arms and legs useless.

The chanting man ended with a flourish and clap of the hands, then drew his broad-bladed knife. Brian's voice rose once more into a heart-rending wail as the man dropped to one knee and gripped the hanging man's hair, yanking his head back to expose the throat. He drew the blade back for a strike—

Carol threw herself back behind the tree, unable to watch. She clapped her hands over her ears, but still heard the instant Brian's pitiable scream was cut off. Her stomach leapt into her throat, but she swallowed it back, breathing hard and fast, using the chill air to try to force her body under control. The bells started again, jingling as the snow squeaked and crunched, and then, as the chanting began anew, there was another sound, a wet *chuck . . . chuck . . . chuck . . .*

She rose to her feet, the back of her coat sliding up the tree as she compelled her shaky legs to obey. Her mind raced faster than her heart, straining for something to do, somewhere to go. She hadn't spotted the road, and it was obvious from their proximity to the village that running through the forest wasn't going to work, even for her. Without the road to lead her, or an open space to run in . . . but she hadn't seen the road: all she had seen from her treetop vantage point had been the village, and—

The idea hit her like a physical thing, her head rocking back against the tree with the simplicity of it. She tensed to run, but knew she had to look first, had to make sure they were still occupied. Still busy. And there was that sound, niggling at the edges of her curiosity, that *chuck . . . chuck* she still heard amid the constant soft jingles. She braced herself and leaned out from the tree, peeking around the trunk.

Two of the red-and-white horrors stood, demonic faces turned toward the sky, arms spread once more in prayer. Between them, the other four crouched about what was left of Brian, blocking his body almost entirely from view; though she couldn't see the man on the ground, the constant jingle of bells came as their feet shifted in the snow with each swing of an arm as the cleavers rose and fell, rose and fell, spraying black arcs onto the snow all about them. Mrs. Barstow's words came back to her: *Your bones for the fire. Your meat for our bellies. Your blood to feed the Stone Mother, and to wake the land.* The snow about the men was soaked with plenty of blood, but it was the rest of what the old woman had said that had Carol's stomach lurching again, as she realized what they were doing in that field.

They were sectioning the meat and bones for easy transport back to the village.

Tears running down her face, hoping their work would take them some time yet, while hating herself *for* that hope, Carol stumbled into a jog. The jog increased to a run, then an all-out sprint as she fled through the trees, not caring if the men heard her, not worrying about snow-covered holes or hidden branches or rocks, just running as fast as she could away from that field of blood and death, toward the only place she could think to go.

CAROL OF THE BELLS

The old woman moved about the great fire, adding a stick here, a log there, keeping the blaze burning evenly, bright flames lighting the whole square. From the look of things, everyone else had returned home to put children to bed, or slip into bed themselves; the square was empty but for the village elder, who paused in her labor, thrusting stick-like hands toward the fire to warm them.

Carol came around the fir at a run, a cast-off length of firewood in one hand, and caught the ancient crone on the side of the head with the makeshift cudgel. With barely a squawk the old woman collapsed into a boneless heap in the well-trodden snow—the same well-trodden snow Carol had remembered the child falling into at the end of the Renewal Dance.

Let 'em try to track me through this, she thought, looking about the empty village square, at the whole festival's worth of footprints marring every inch of snow she could see. She knew she only had minutes, however, before her pursuers followed her back and let the villagers know she was among them. A house-to-house search and she would be found quickly enough—found and butchered in the same square she now stood in.

If she were still here, that is.

I'm screwed if Brian had his keys in his pocket. She ran across the square toward the Earle's Inn, the rented Saab still parked out front. *But if he left them on the dresser or something, I'm driving the hell out of here.*

She slipped up the steps to the porch, boots clomping lightly on the wood, praying the door would still be unlocked. The heavy portal swung open at her touch, revealing the shadowy taproom, as empty as she'd left it a mere two hours earlier; it felt like a lifetime ago. She paused, listening to the house, alert for the scrape of foot on floorboard, the tread of shoe on stair, or—God forbid—the jingle of bells, no matter how soft.

Nothing.

She crept toward the stairs leading up to their room, nervously clutching the rough club with which she had felled the old woman, ears peeled for the slightest sound. She had just reached the door when she heard it.

The faint jingle of bells.

She whipped half about, looking back toward the front door—and was taken completely by surprise when the door to the stairs burst open right in front of her with a sudden loud jingle. The swinging door caught the tip of her stick, knocking it from her hand as she staggered back with a terrified shout, and the open doorway was suddenly filled with the hulking form of one of the red-and-white hunters. The huge demonic face stared at her, stone-toothed mouth frozen in a hungry snarl, the creature's hands splayed with surprise. Carol hesitated, frozen with fear and indecision: go for the club or turn and run? But the heavy front door was closed behind her, and she'd never make it through before this monster was upon her with knife and cleaver. She'd already shifted her weight forward, her body responding before any conscious decision, starting a desperate dive for the club, when, as if in answer to her thoughts, the hunter's hand darted toward the knife at his belt.

Carol's heart shriveled. *Too late!*

Then the killer fumbled his weapon and sent it tumbling to the floor.

Already in motion, Carol made a split-second decision and went for the knife. She caught up the handle with both hands and rose from her crouch, swiftly thrusting the blade between them in a terrified *en garde* position. Raising her eyes to the hunter as she came up from the floor, she saw his great mask swiveling as he looked for his weapon—then suddenly he went for the club at Carol's feet, not even glancing her way as he moved.

As the hunter dove forward, Carol's rising knife came up under the chin of the mask, and the man impaled himself with all the power of her legs driving up and all the force of his body dropping down. The razor-sharp steel slid into the underside of his chin, flesh providing no more resistance than water, until the hilt slammed home under the big man's jaw. Carol's wrists struck the bottom edge of the mask, knocking it upward and off, flipping away into the stairwell beyond. Carol released the knife, staggering back in horror.

Simon Barstow stared at her, knife-hilt sprouting from the underside of his chin like some stylish beard, the entire blade buried in his flesh and bone and brain. He took a half step forward, staring at her with frightened eyes, and raised a trembling hand in her direction. Though no sound came, his lips formed a single word before a gush of red ran down his chin

(Mum?)

and with a loud clatter of bells he fell, sprawling face down on the rough floorboards.

Jesus Christ. Her lips shaped the words without voice as she backed away from the body, horrified by these people, this place, and what she had done, nearly covering her face with her hands before realizing they were red and sticky, gloved with Simon's cooling blood. Her stomach clenched, lurched, and its contents, so long held in check through sheer force of will, spattered on the taproom floor.

Suddenly the door behind the bar flew open, Mrs. Barstow bustling through with a rack of clean glasses in her hands.

"Now, Simon, all I been hearing all night is them bells. I told you to take off—" She froze at the sight of Carol standing in the dim taproom, eyes widening magnificently in surprise.

"You," she said, the word not much more than a puff of breath, then raised her voice to its more familiar, strident level. "Simon! I need—"

Her eyes focused on the body sprawled on the floor. The red-and-white clothing. The bells at knees and ankles. The spreading pool of blood. The glasses hit the floor with a splintering *crash* as she staggered forward to catch hold of the bar top, staring open-mouthed.

"Si—Simon?" The whisper was unbelieving and unfocused. "What did she . . . what did she do to . . ."

Her eyes, terrible and burning with hate, swung about to fix upon Carol, already backing toward the door, and her next words cut the air like a rage-filled steam whistle.

"*What did you do to my son?*"

The question was flung at Carol's back as she sprinted through the door and into the night. She passed the Saab without a thought, starting for the road out of town, when lights flashed on in the house ahead of her. Then the one next to that. Then two more across the square, as she staggered to a halt. Upstairs lights, bedroom lights as people about the village woke to the wailing of Mrs. Barstow, screamed threats filling the air.

"We'll kill you! You won't just wake the Land; you'll take a long time to die! *I'll wield the knife myself!*"

Carol looked left and right as more lights flicked to life, the helpless feeling of a trapped animal overtaking her; for a moment she felt as she thought Brian must have felt, speaking with a voice already dead as they stumbled beneath the trees. Exhausted from running through the snow, wounded and bleeding, she knew there was no way she could escape on foot from the entire roused village.

Just no way.

Then she heard it: the bright jingle and *chink-chink-chink* of bell-laden boots at a dead sprint. The hunters were coming, the butchers bringing back half of the solstice feast meat. Her body, already twitching with exhaustion, got a fresh shot of adrenaline, screaming for her to *Go! Go! Go!*

She'd taken a single step in the direction of the road when the voice floated from somewhere in the trees, powerful and deep though out of breath.

"Mary! Mary, what is it, lass? Mary!"

Mr. Barstow, running hell-for-leather toward his screaming wife, the hunt forgotten in his fear for his family. The fact of this registered somewhere deep within Carol a moment or two before she knew she understood it, and she was already in motion toward the fire even as the plan occurred to her. She was aware of the screaming woman, the shouting man, and especially of those bells pounding closer through the trees, but she blocked it all out and focused on *moving*.

A half-dozen strides brought her to the edge of the bonfire, where she pivoted and sprinted back toward the inn, a burning brand in each hand. The steam-whistle voice still blasted through the open inn door in waves separated by sobbing.

"We'll take your blood! I'll eat your heart!"

"Fuck you, you crazy *bitch*!" she screamed, flinging one, then the other of the flaming torches in through the open doorway. There was a *fwumph* as something went up in flames, and the screams from inside degenerated into a single long, wordless shriek.

"*Mary*!" Oliver Barstow came roaring out from between two of the houses lining the square, mask missing, eyes wild, bells stabbing the air with every stride. Carol, running toward the fire again, swerved away as he passed. He spared her not a glance, staggering on toward his screaming wife and their burning home.

There were more shouts from the forest, more bells signaling the hunting party drawing near, though none of them had been able to keep pace with Barstow once the fear had hit him. Carol ran to and from the fire, the stink of smoke surrounding her, embers burning her fingers raw as she grabbed hunks of flame to hurl at the surrounding houses. Some merely struck walls and bounced off, sizzling as they plopped into the snow, while others landed on porches, guttering against the boards in the dark. Some precious few, though, smashed through glass and muntin to be caught neatly by the thick curtains that were a staple in any home with single-pane glass and cold winters. The curtains, dry from weeks of holding back icy drafts, took the flame as easily as any well-laid tinder, and the light streaming through the broken windows grew as the fire spread, the air filling with the shouts of men, and the screams of women and children.

By the time the rest of the hunting party came crashing out of the woods, tongues of fire licked up from the broken windows and out the open doors as some of the families fled out into the snow. The red-and-white-clad hunters ignored Carol, not even seeing her as they ran, focused on the fires and their own families. As Carol made her way toward the road once more, Mary and Oliver Barstow struggled out of the inn, dragging Simon's great bulk between them. Villagers were fighting the flames in their neighbor's homes and had no time for the inn, and the wood-and-whiskey-filled taproom had become an inferno.

As Carol passed, they lay their son on his back in the snow, the knife-hilt jutting up at an obscene angle from beneath his chin. Oliver Barstow's hands fluttered over the hilt, as if wanting to pull the knife free but unable to force himself to do so. Mary Barstow glanced up just as Carol moved through her field of vision, and the women locked eyes. The older woman bared her teeth, and Carol thought she might actually be hissing. She broke into a jog, keeping watch on the Barstows over her shoulder.

"There she is!" the missus screamed, slapping the mister on the shoulder, trying to drive him to his feet. "Go after her!" Oliver Barstow, however, did not react, kneeling over his son and weeping, hands still fluttering. Carol increased her pace to a run, trying to get out of sight before the crowd managed to put any of the fires out and had time to think of anything else—like finding the one who'd started them.

"We'll find you!" the strident, hate-filled voice followed Carol up the road as she increased her pace yet again. "You can run, but you can't hide, you murdering bitch! We'll find you wherever you run to! We will find you!"

Carol ignored the threats and epithets, put the terrible, burning village at her back, found her pace on the relatively smooth, cleared road, and she ran . . . and ran . . . and ran.

"And I'm sorry, but that's all I can tell you."

"But really, miss, that's nothing more that you told us yesterday."

"I know," said Carol. "I did say I was sorry. Don't you think *I* want them caught? I wouldn't mind if the whole bunch was *dead*, never mind in jail!" She gnawed her lip as the detective inspector flipped his notebook to the beginning with a sigh and began to read his notes back to her.

"A motorist found you running by the side of a road . . . somewhere. Brought you to a small town; you're not sure of the name. You opted not to go to hospital, but began hitchhiking your way toward London, accepting about a half-dozen rides over the course of a day and a half, until you got to Swindon, where someone finally noticed you were bleeding and dropped you here at the Great Western Hospital. You"—he sighed again, then cleared his throat—"came in on one of the M roads, though you're not sure which one, the M4, M5, or M40, and also on one of the A roads, though you're not certain what number or numbers there, either, though you think you were moving in a generally eastward direction."

He flipped the notebook closed and rubbed his forehead for a moment.

"Which means, basically," he said, finally, "that even if you have your direction of travel correct, that simply narrows it down to everything to the west, northwest, and north of Swindon—which includes about ninety percent of England, and all of Wales. You're certain you have no idea where you were?"

Carol's shoulders rose defensively. "Hey, it's not my fault you named all your roads the same way! How the hell does anyone keep track?"

"But when you were *going* to this village—you said Brian Freeman had gotten directions, knew where you were going?"

"Yes. He did. *I* was just along for the ride."

"And you don't know what this village is called?"

"I told you, we were just traveling from village to village. After a while they all started to blend together."

The detective inspector asked a few more questions, and though Carol answered them as best she could, fighting tears some of the time, she saw how little help she was actually being by the growing annoyance in the man's eyes. He maintained his polite tone, however, even going so far as to stay with her through the discharge process and walk her out of the hospital.

"Clean bill of health, then?"

"Clean enough," she said. "The hip didn't need any stitches, and other than that the most painful thing is the burns to my hands, but even they're going to be fine—or so I'm told."

"Yes," said the detective inspector as they walked through the hospital foyer and out to the sidewalk. "You were lucky. You're taking the train to London?"

"Yep. My father's meeting me there to take me home just as soon as we can get a flight. No offense, but . . ." she remembered Mrs. Barstow's screamed threats—*We'll find you wherever you run to! We will find you!*—and shuddered. "I plan to get as far from your country as I can, just as fast as I can."

He offered her a sympathetic look, having listened to her story twice. He walked to the police car parked at the curb and opened the rear door with a bit of flourish.

"Well, the least I can do is offer you a ride to the station. Merry Christmas, miss."

Carol started in surprise, then smiled. "That's right, this *is* Christmas, isn't it? Thank you, I'd—"

The morning air was suddenly shattered by the bright, shivery tinkle of jingling bells. The small bag of belongings she had collected over the past three days hit the pavement with a thud that no one heard as, with a blood-curdling screech, Carol Friday turned and pelted down the sidewalk.

She never saw the detective inspector exchange a glance with the man standing by his red Salvation Army kettle, fistful of sleigh bells in hand for attracting the attention of passersby. She never saw the policeman run after her, never heard him calling her name or shouting for her to stop. She didn't see anything but the open space before her, didn't hear anything but the bells behind her as she ran . . . and ran . . . and ran.

About the Author

Rob Smales is the author of dozens of short stories, the collection *Echoes of Darkness*, the novella *Friends in High Places*, and identifies as a dad, writer, editor, and postal worker—in that order.

To find out more about him, you can look him up on Facebook or check out his website at www.RobSmales.com.

If you liked Carol of the Bells, try Friends in High Places!

He just wanted friends

He pestered them day after day to be considered one of the guys, but they didn't want anything to do with him. They ignored and made fun of him, ditching him at every opportunity, but Tommy wouldn't take the hint.

They came up with a plan to drive him away.

It was only a harmless prank

In order to be accepted, Tommy would have to pass an initiation and face his worst fear. They were certain he'd chicken out, but he accepted the challenge.

That's when it all went wrong.

If only they hadn't left him

The ambulances wouldn't have come.

The police wouldn't be asking so many questions.

And maybe Tommy wouldn't still be following them.

Also by Rob Smales: LaundryLegs

Old Mr. Ross didn't believe in LaundryLegs. He thought the monstrous centipede was made up by his wife—a joke to scare their kids. But after his wife's death, Mr. Ross finds himself face-to-face with the creature.

Or does he?

Stricken with grief over the loss of his wife, and fearful of his looming mental decline, Mr. Ross begins to doubt his own sanity. Is the monster in his basement real? Is it an alcohol-fueled nightmare?

Or is he losing his mind?

Coming Soon: Spearfinger

EXTRA! EXTRA!
READ ALL ABOUT IT!
People—children—in Cherokee, North Carolina, are dying.
Murdered.
The police say things are under control, but the death toll is climbing.
Enter Carl Spaberg, ace reporter: legend in his own mind.
Carl doesn't know why his bosses have sent him to Cherokee, nor does he care. Recently blackballed down to *tabloid* status, Carl only wants one thing: to break a story so big and juicy it'll catapult him back into the big leagues—and he's not going to let a little thing like the truth stand in his way.
But when the case involves an obnoxious investigator, the world's oldest car thief, and a thousand-year-old ogress, isn't it possible the truth may actually be stranger than fiction?
Beware the thunder!

Don't miss out!

Visit the website below and you can sign up to receive emails whenever Rob Smales publishes a new book. There's no charge and no obligation.

https://books2read.com/r/B-A-SGWU-VVXGC

Connecting independent readers to independent writers.